The
TIME
TOUCHER

Clare McAndrew

First published in Great Britain as a softback original in 2017

Copyright © Clare McAndrew

The moral right of this author has been asserted.

All rights reserved.

All characters and events in this book, other than those clearly in the public domain, are fictitious and any resemblance to real persons, living or dead, is purely coincidental.

No part of this publication may be reproduced, stored in a retrieval system, or transmitted, in any form or by any means, without the prior permission in writing of the publisher, nor be otherwise circulated in any form of binding or cover other than that in which it is published and without a similar condition including this condition being imposed on the subsequent purchaser.

Typeset in Alegreya

Editing, design, typesetting and publishing by UK Book Publishing

www.ukbookpublishing.com

ISBN: 978-1-912183-02-9

A Serene Silence

The mystical waves gently caressing the elder rocks, as if

To wash away centuries of turmoil in the sea.

The angelic waves of a native bird dancing a secret dance mid-air, whispering, waltzing, wishing.

The sea mist breathing a gush of life over the stillness of the day.

The gently blown grass swaying to and fro reluctant to decide its fate.

The dazzling, shimmering reflections gazing back like the mirrors of our souls from the mesmerising rock pools.

It was timeless

It was endless

Captured;

In a split moment of time

In the blink of an eye

In the skip of a heart beat

This was our moment in time.

Dedication

To My Family and Friends

Thank you for a lifetime of love and laughter. Memories which fill my heart and make me feel so lucky each day. You say I have never really grown up and that I still live in my own little world of fairy tales, that I see the world and the people in it through rose tinted glasses. But what a wonderful world I see. Open your eyes, your heart and look for the magic – it's out there. Just smile and the world will smile with you. Take a chance and join me. Phoebe, Austin and Jenson, I wish you a lifetime of fun, thrills and adventure; never be afraid to follow your dreams.

You have but one life, a life of untouched experiences and hidden pathways...

A life of love, wishes and dreams...

Live your life, don't be afraid, for yours is here right now, today.

Perhaps tomorrow...

Enriched in the warmth of the summer sun my soul flies free.

Beckoned by the timeless blue sky, the thrill of life seduces me.

Think not of whom? What? When? Or why?

I have no regrets, no need to cry.

My heart it races in timeless glee,

Until the day you are here with me.

Forever in my heart until that one inevitable day I shout...
Fly me to the moon! It's been an incredible ride.

The TIME TOUCHER

Chapter One

What if?

Have you ever wondered what if?

What if the moon really was made of cheese?

What if pigs really could fly?

And what if you actually took that risk, grasped fate with both hands and carried out that childhood dream of sending that message in a bottle?

Well, that is exactly what I decided to do. As a young child I never hid away from challenges. I was never afraid to enter into the unknown and I was always first to take a chance. Each day I saw as a new adventure, a new experience, a chance to make a new memory.

It was a typical Sunday morning; I had woken up particularly early that day. I had the faded recollection of having some weird dream, something about symbols and I had the uneasy feeling that I should remember more, that it had some kind of importance to me. Nevertheless the alarm on my phone was not set but my internal alarm was. It was half past six and the birds were singing; with the rays of sunlight shining in the gaps of the fuchsia pink bedroom curtains I lay deep in thought. I tried to re-enact the dream in my mind, trying to put the obscure pieces together, trying to make sense of it but it was no good: all I could vaguely remember was its importance. It felt real. As I lay there I tried to shift the unnerving feeling I had and smiled in realisation – thankfully it was the start of the school holidays. Yeah I had to do revision for upcoming exams, but I was also looking forward to going to stay with my grandparents for a few days.

It's on early mornings like these I start to question my life and decisions. Having chosen my subject options only a couple of years earlier the time had crept up on me and I had to start thinking about my future. I felt nervous, jittery and wondered when was that moment in time that had changed me from the brave little girl I was into this quivering shadow? Who was that 16 year old teenager who looked back at me from the mirror every day?

Maybe it was all the stress and decisions I had to make and then there was school! All the exams I was preparing for, all those revision classes every night or having to choose my subject options for my A levels. Everyone was asking, "What do you want to be when you're older?" I guess I was just scared to be spontaneous anymore, I felt I had to grow up quickly and now that Mum and Dad were getting divorced I guess I was in the real world now and no more living in my own Disney Princess world.

Well, that day I had made my mind up: today I would try and find her, open that wardrobe door and step back into Narnia. I would dance with the fairies, play with the pixies and live each moment with the passion and excitement that had evaded my life for so long.

Putting on my bath robe I walked into the bathroom. Ritual, pulling back the shower curtain, any spiders lurking in the bath? No...check.

Turn on the shower, fiddle with the hot and cold taps, listen to the gurgling, check water just right...check.

Gown thrown onto the barely warm radiator, I stepped into the warm inviting shower. This time it was different, the water seemed to wash away my fears, almost cleanse my whole being. I felt invigorated, alive, bursting with exuberance. I was excited; today was a new day, a new beginning, a new me or maybe the day I would find the old me.

Opening the wardrobe door I had a sudden flutter, a spine tickling moment and butterflies in my tummy. "Narnia," I spoke out loud. Glancing through my abundance of dresses hanging like different personas to mimic my different moods each day, I settled on a pretty white cotton summer dress. Clean, fresh and embroidered with beautiful intricate lace, reminiscent of the lace my Nan had dotted around her home, underneath her jewellery box, under her favourite vase and my favourite on the collar of her favourite pink blouse. It appeared in all forms, in many places. I thought back and a smile came to my face and a warm glow embraced my body, oh how I loved her so.

Next, shoes. "Hmm," I stuttered. Well I needed to be comfortable – after all I was going to go the beach as soon as I dropped my case off at Nan's. Waterproof too and, above all else of course, fashionable! Not the kind of sandals I recalled being forced to wear as a child. "Hey Peppermint Patty," the kids would shout as I walked around in the most ghastly but very practical summer sandals. I hated them.

"These are perfect, you won't get bunions or crooked feet with these," my mum had said. Bunions and crooked feet would have been a welcome exchange for the cruel jibes and constant name calling I had to endure every day at primary school for wearing them. Peppermint Patty was a cartoon character from a TV programme which was popular in those days, unfortunately for me. She was the kind of character you wouldn't want to be compared to. She had freckles, a mop of dull and unkempt mousey brown hair styled in a home cut basin type cut. A real tomboy with ghastly dress sense and of courses those sandals. Brown leather sandals, a single leather strap, no pretty design just very plain and very practical.

Thankfully, Mum had mellowed or maybe it was just that she was far too busy with her new job, new boyfriend and new life to go shoe shopping for me anymore. It was now a case of money is on the bench, food is in the fridge and if your dad calls round don't forget to tell him he owes me for this and that!

So after much thought and after trying on my new 'Vans' I decided on a pair of pink and white lace plimsolls. Very pretty with threads of pink and lilac and embossed with the outlines of daisies. No Peppermint Patty for me.

Next was to pick a suitable bag, something big enough to carry on my train journey necessities but again something that would look smart draped on my shoulder swaying elegantly against my summer dress.

All of a sudden my eyes were attracted to something

shimmering, gently glistening like the delicate glow of a glow worm sleeping in a deep trance. Pulling it from the shelf I realised it was a Star and Moon zip charm which was attached to the perfect bag. An exquisite charm made of silver and mother of pearl. The moon, if you looked really carefully you could see the craters, different colours and swirls of opaque, silver and crystallised brown. It looked as if it was really a piece of the moon and I loved it.

Grabbing my notebook and my pink Swarovski pen that I had got as a present from my best friend Phoebe, I put them into my bag. All I needed was an empty coca cola plastic bottle and I was ready to test fate.

Phoebe and I had been friends since nursery school. She was and still is the most beautiful girl you have ever seen. Green almond shaped eyes, tanned skin and long, flowing, shiny brown hair. If she stepped into a room people would stop talking and stare; walking down the street you would see drivers looking out their car windows at her. My mum would say, "Youse two will stop traffic one day." Well I don't know about me but Phoebe definitely did and she was always totally humble and shy about her good looks too. She was also the cleverest girl in year 11 expecting A star grade in every subject. She was my best friend I could tell her anything and she would always be there for me, like the sister I had never had. She always had a way of making everything feel fine and we always had a laugh together.

She would say in the voice of a mature and well lived, wise 50 year old, "Change is a good thing, Cassie, it's exciting!"

Well little did I know it but my life was about to change that week and things would never be the same again.

After breakfast and answering my texts from my mates I decided to go to the local shop and pick up a magazine for the journey. Yeah I had my 'Bose' headphones and I had just downloaded some of my favourite songs from iTunes but I liked to have a couple of magazines to break up the time and more importantly I needed that plastic coca cola bottle.

It was a beautiful summer morning. The street was awake with the hustle and bustle of its inhabitants scurrying about their day. Old Bob across the street waved as he struggled to control the lawn mower with only one hand. "Morning Cassie, lovely day," he shouted over. He was always such a happy man, always had a huge smile on his face and was always the first to offer a hand to any old lady or elderly neighbour, despite the fact he was probably the oldest person on the street. Further down the street was Faye, a new mum with twins and a puppy. I watched as she happily strode up the lane, power walking with the twin pram intent on losing those post-pregnancy pounds. She was a really pretty girl, elf-like petite features, dazzling blue eyes and a kind of aura surrounded her, making everyone want to be in her presence. Let's just say she had that elusive quality, she had the X factor. Not too far behind her was Warren, her betrothed, a slender and slight framed young man with the physique of a cyclist. Skinny legs, not much of a bottom and always in a hurry. This morning was no different: he soon caught up to his family, puppy in tow. The puppy was a not-so-welcome addition to the street for most, barking at 6am every morning; the neighbours didn't take kindly to the canine capers.

I, on the other hand, loved it; I always did love dogs. When most people got broody over newborn babies I got broody over doe eyed puppies and this time was no exception.

"Hi Faye, Warren, perfect day to take the boys out," I said as I bent over the pram to acknowledge their pride and joys. Warren was beaming with a hint of over exaggerated masculinity – after all he had fathered twins and strapping young bruisers they were too.

I then, on bended knee, greeted Mia, my idea of a

perfect bundle of joy although today she looked more like a perfect bundle of fluff. A walking cotton wool ball eagerly came towards me, sniffing and yelping with pure excitement. Mia was a little bichon frise, a pedigree breed which apparently originated from Spain and were closely linked to the favourite breeds of royalty. She was only 12 weeks old and this was one of her first outings. Her brushed out coat was more like candyfloss than hair and her perfect eyes were like chocolate buttons only with an adventurous sparkle.

Her pretty little face and excited stance made my heart jump. "I've no treats for you this morning, Mia," I said, feeling guilty. Must remember buy some dog treats, I made a mental note to go with the thousands of other mental notes which once made would disappear into the abyss.

Outside the shop were some kids from school, standing with energy drinks in their hands and trying unsuccessfully to bottle flip. Peter, the red haired one, kicked his friend's bottle and it burst, leaking the syrupy contents all over the path. Something made me look at the river of juice as it swirled and made a pattern, a familiar shape; familiar, yeah it was, but from where? I recalled seeing it before but I couldn't remember. Anyway it was spilled juice! What was I watching it for? Then as if to break me from my trance I heard a voice call my name.

"Hi Cassie," said Austin, a really good looking lad in my year. Austin was a really nice lad with gorgeous big blue eyes and surfer like blonde wispy hair. He was a keen footballer and played for our local team and he had been scouted by someone and was now playing for a premiership academy. He wasn't up himself or a player, he was a genuine nice person. He was always laughing, a bit of a joker but he was really kind and friends with everyone really popular and I had a secret crush on him.

"What you up to?" he said smiling and making me have butterflies in my tummy. The other guys were just messing on; one was doing the stupid craze at the moment called 'The dab', flying his arms over his head in a sharp movement and in truth looking like the eejit he really is. Another guy was playing some game on his phone and after nearly falling off the pavement he stumbled, knocking his mate, which was the excuse they needed to start fun fighting! "Honestly they are in year 11 now not year 7!" I uttered underneath my breath.

I realised Austin was still waiting for a reply and I smiled and told him I was on my way to stay with my grandparents for a week of the Easter holidays.

His face dropped as he nodded and he gave a half-hearted smile. "Shame, you could have come with US; we are going to the cinema today then for a burger at 'The Old Pot'."

"Us" I thought to myself – well he wasn't exactly asking me out on a date but then again his face did drop when he realised I wouldn't be able to go. "Yeah, another time," I replied, brushing my long hair from my face and tucking it behind my ear. I had watched a programme about how to flirt and the actress did this, probably nothing like the way I had done it but I thought it was worth a try.

Walking past him and making a conscious effort not to look back I walked into the shop and started to browse through the magazines. There was no one else in the shop except the owner and I wondered if he could hear my heart pounding, my blood racing through my body as I thought about Austin.

As I walked back home my tummy started to churn and made a grumbling noise – it was that mention of 'The Old Pot', a lovely little coffee shop in town.

I had been going there for as long as I could remember, since being a small girl with my mum. It was such a warm and friendly place, it felt like having lunch with your family or at your favourite aunt and uncle's. All the staff were lovely, always laughing and having a joke. It was great because even before Mum and I would order they would always know exactly what we wanted and they were like this with everyone. The owner was such a happy, fun-loving chap, baldy head, rosy cheeks and an infectious smile that welcomed everyone in from the cold, invited them to rest their feet and tempted them with real home-cooked traditional food. He did a lot of fundraising for charity, donating money to the local hospital. He also provided a meals on wheels service for the elderly folk and every day he would give them their home cooked, fresh, hot dinners. Mince and dumplings, Sunday roasts, whatever the special of the day was and followed by the best I had ever tasted, lumpy, moreish rice pudding that had been cooked in the pan. Of course what he really was providing wasn't just the food, it was a regular visit, regular laugh, chat and smile that brightened their day and made them feel like someone did care, they were not alone. A nice man with a big heart.

Chapter Two

*Somewhere down the road will be
an answer to your question.*

With all my bags packed, magazine, my mobile phone and my favourite beany toy, I was off to the train station, ready to embark on a new adventure. 'Beanie' was a dirty yellow, plush velvet doll with an equally dirty plastic face. I had had her for as long as I can remember. Beanie's tummy was full of beans – well, I say beans but actually I'm not sure what she was full of and I guess I will never know. I do know, however, she was squidgy and squashy and full of love. She was only as big as the palm of my hand but she was perfect. Her small delicate face, pink rosy cheeks and little button nose was worn with kisses of time. She came with me everywhere, sleepovers, holidays, my forever friend.

I said my farewells to the goldfish Pepe and Pippin

and got into my mum's car; phew it was hot in there. Opening the windows, I glanced at the side mirror just as a little spider hurriedly crawled back behind it. It was a nice feeling really. Although I was terrified of spiders I felt good knowing that Mum was in some way providing a home for them, albeit behind her wing mirror and out of my view.

My mind drifted for a moment as I thought back and I smiled, remembering the fun, the great adventures and all the exciting times I had spent as a young child with my great grandad David, my grandad Brian and my Nan each school holiday. A tear entered my eye, my heart suddenly felt very heavy; my great grandad had passed two years earlier. I guess I was lucky really, I was sixteen and I had been lucky enough to spend 14 years of my life with him. Some of the other kids in my class hadn't even met their grandads let alone their great-grandads because they had died sometimes before they were born or when they were very small and had no memory of meeting them. The emptiness and longing had stayed with me each day. The pain of my loss and the sadness it brought had tinged my very soul and was a constant unwelcome visitor; it never got easier.

Friends would say time would heal my pain but it never did. Every anniversary, every birthday or every special life event I wanted to share with him I was left with an incurable longing and a vast void. Simple things really. Just being able to tell him a new fact I had learned, discuss an archaeological discovery that I knew he would have been interested in, or simply just for him to be there and share my life. I remembered thinking about him in last week's assembly. We had visitors in from a local church organisation and we were all asked to complete an anonymous survey and write down 'What hurts most'. Some of the boys in my class thought it would be funny to write down "when I am playing football and I get hit in the balls!"; others wrote about when their parents had split up or when they had fallen out with their best friends. Some kids had mentioned when they were being bullied or called names, others about when they had lost a pet. Funny thing was though, everyone wrote something, unlike most of the time when we get asked to complete mind numbing surveys at school. The most popular reply by far was losing a loved one.

To me what hurt most was losing him.

I missed him terribly, missed his warmth, missed his unwavering support and missed, more than anything in the whole wide world, his smile. A smile that could light up the whole room. A smile that could brighten up the darkest of days. A smile that always told me no matter what, everything was going to be alright. Wiping away a tear, I smiled because I knew. I knew I was truly loved.

The car still felt like a glass greenhouse that day. The gauge showed 20 degrees. The dashboard looked extra dusty and the air was filled with floating particles, dancing in front of my eyes until they settled, making little patterns, gently kissing the once shiny interior and landing, making an all too familiar symbol.

My daydream was suddenly interrupted when I glanced at something out of the corner of my eye. I watched as a butterfly glided past, almost waving as it quickly changed its course.

With elegant moves it appeared to be auditioning for a part on one of those TV shows. Its wings were burnt orange in colour, with edges of subtle golden hues. The wings had wisps of delicate amber threads running through, entwined together in a delicate spider web like pattern. It floated past intent on a new direction, a new route, a new path, all leading to an exciting and new destination.

Reaching down, Mum flicked through her bundle of CDs, settling on one.

The first track began, "Somewhere down the road there will be answers to the questions", and how pertinent Faith Hill's lyrics were. "They will have the answers at the end of the road." I thought about the butterfly again, how it had suddenly changed direction, its destiny. I never knew how alike we were. I was about to open my wings, changing my direction in life too, and fulfil my destiny.

The car journey passed fairly quickly as I was entertained by my mum singing along to her CD. She was a good singer and she loved to tell me the stories of how she was once a backing singer for a famous musician when she was a young girl, before she had me. I had bought her the new CD as a gift; I was supposed to be saving to go to a music festival with Phoebe and the other girls at school but I couldn't resist buying it. I couldn't really resist buying loads of things really, lol. My friends and I had gone the week before to the city and had great fun shopping and trying on different outfits. It was hilarious; each one of us would choose an outfit for each other, something totally gross and make each other try it on. We would have such a laugh taking selfie photographs and uploading them on Facebook. I did need a couple of new things because I was going to the local annual fun fair when I got back from my grandparents' and everyone would be there. It was the kind of event where it was important to look good, without looking like you were trying to! So I had bought some lush faded denim ripped jeans and a white off the shoulder top.

After all, Austin would be there.

Pulling up in the railway station car park I glanced up, looking at the big ornate Victorian clock. It was very prominent, up high on the old stone wall. Not long before my train I felt a sudden rush, a flutter of excitement racing through my veins and an all-encompassing surge of heat through my entire body. Winding down the car window I gasped, breathing in the distinct, fresh, cooling air. I welcomed the gentle breeze delicately brushing my cheek and cooling me down. I could feel my eyes sparkling and widening in anticipation and in the sudden realisation that I was finally here. I was finally ready to board the train, it felt like I was going home, yes it was not my real home but the one place in the entire world where my heart was, where I had spent my happiest of times and where I belonged.

It was a place I had spent so many fun filled days as a young girl with my Nan and Grandad or Pops as I liked to call him. I found that these last couple of years I rarely visited as much; life and my teenage years had taken over. The place had always filled me with intrigue, it was a place of fantasy and mystique, and it was a place where dreams could come true.

Stepping out of the car I made my way to the platform. I looked around to see if I recognised anybody but I didn't. The hanging baskets, however, looked in full bloom: glorious flowers with colours of purples, blues and pinks welcomed me. I immediately felt at ease, relaxed and happy as I sat on the green metal station bench and listened to the general chit chatter of the locals with their quaint lovable accent. Suddenly all my thoughts and worries about my GCSE exams had left my head as the train pulled up and I gave Mum a hug goodbye.

Chapter Three

Tempus Fugit (Time Flies)

My grandfather or Pops as I liked to call him was such an amazing man. He was so adventurous and exciting and had lots of interesting tales and stories to tell. He was well known in the village and was an easily recognisable character. Everyone knew him as the old man in the cap, a distinctive green tweed cap that he happened to wear most days. It was no ordinary cap, it was very special. It had been given to him as a Thank you gift from a milliner who had made the exact same cap by Royal Commission for a member of the Royal Family. Olive green in colour with wisps of emerald and aubergine threads remarkably gliding through it. A small but delicate feather rested at the side. Crimson and royal blue in colour, from an obscure bird with an even more obscure name.

Pops had lived in the village most of his life and

relished in anything traditional. He had traced his family name way back and although it was not from local descent he was still extremely proud of his heritage and his ancestors.

His coat of arms, set on a wall plaque, took pride of place above the old fireplace. The words 'Tempus Fugit' (time flies) inscribed below. An image of a glove from a medieval warrior grasping a golden goblet shone from up high, almost as if to triumphantly give a toast to life itself.

Brew, where he and Nan lived, was a small, traditional coastal village but with a sense of heritage and history like no other place I have seen. One of my favourite places to visit was 'Station Books', set in the remains of what had been an old train station. The building had been converted into a great secondhand book shop. The walls were made of light coloured stones which held in place the original stone arches supporting the ornate and intricate chequered glass stained windows. There were fancy green iron posts in place attaching each wall to another with metal swirls and filigree petals frozen in mid-air. There were shelves and shelves of books, all different genres, different sizes and in different states of repair. The shelves were numbered A1 to Z2 and the wealth of knowledge within them was outstanding. There were circular tables dotted around for people to just come and sit and read, contemplate, relax and enjoy the magical ambience of the place. It was the kind of bookshop you would expect to see in 'Hogwarts'. With Harry Potter sitting reading in the corner. Running along the specially made delft rack up high in the eaves was an old model tin train. Red and green in colour with three little carriages of old English cream, chuntering around the heavens, breaking the stillness of the silence with its occasional toot. From the quaint coffee shop which was the original waiting room, it was easy to look around and imagine what it was like in bygone years. The walls were olive green in colour plastered in the original thin, shiny tiles. The floors were made from solid wooden floorboards which have had many steps weather them throughout the years but still with their light worn patches and deep set grooves and scars they preserved its history for all to see. I loved to sit on the old wooden church like pew benches and enjoy my favourite lemon drizzle cake and hot pink lemonade as Pops munched on a traditional fruit and oat bake.

As I fingered through the books, I would pick one out that took my fancy, open it and notice the smudged fingerprints on the old, well-read pages. My imagination would go into overdrive as I thought about all the people who had read the books before me – what were their stories? Each one would have a different journey, a different life and a different fate; each one would be as unique as their smudged fingerprints but each one would have one thing in common... the book.

The train journey seemed quicker than usual, maybe that is because there were lots of people to watch and keep me amused. Yes, you have guessed it, I'm a people watcher – what girl isn't at the age of 16 – I am fascinated by everyone's little idiosyncrasies and their odd habits. I was sitting on a seat with a table which is always really good because you can put your packed lunch on it and your iPad or one of those fancy 'grown up' colouring in books and coloured pens that are all the fashion these days. The only bad thing with this is when you are travelling alone you really do not know who you will have siting opposite you. On this occasion I was really lucky: it was a very sweet old lady. She had a very cheerful and happy round face and wore a long pink and purple raincoat. Underneath she had a maroon coloured woolly cardigan with the perfect amount of buttons to play 'Tinker, Tailor, and Soldier...' Of course as long as you end up counting eight buttons – after all, every young girl wants to marry a 'Rich' man.

A somewhat majestic man with a great aura of

benevolence about him came towards me. He had immaculate brown Italian leather polished shoes. His shoes were so shiny you could see your reflection in them. His laces were tied in an intricate but perfectly symmetric bow. He was dressed in a very light coloured, distinguished designer suit. It had very thin pinstripes which added to its regality and he had a pretty silk handkerchief in his jacket pocket with the initials BJR embroidered on it and a motif. In his hand was a newspaper and draped over his arm a camel coloured overcoat. I tried to make it not obvious by staring but I was keen to see what the motif was because again it looked familiar.

"Thank you, you're very kind," said the old lady, eager to sit down and rest her weary feet as the man lifted her suitcase onto the rack above her seat.

"You're very welcome, petal," said the man, smiling with the smile of a distinguished older gentleman.

He then looked at me, an inquisitive sixteen year old and smiled; there was something odd about his stance. "Does this belong to you?" he said, holding out his hand. I noticed he was wearing brown leather gloves, finely stitched with a criss-cross pattern along the edges. It was very odd, it was a scorching hot day and he was wearing gloves? Opening his clenched fist lay my special pen, set free as if it had been somehow imprisoned by his strong grip.

"You ok, flower?" he said.

"Yes, thank you, I'm fine," I replied. "Yes it is my pen, thank you, I had not realised I had dropped it." I couldn't even remember taking it out of my bag, in fact I'm positive I had not used it. Then again I suppose I must have done if he had found it on the floor. He smiled again, then looking directly into my eyes he nodded and then left, just wandering further down the carriage. I had the feeling that he knew something and he was not telling me. It was very strange. It was very odd.

Going back to his own seat, he sat down with the knowledge he had done yet another good deed that day, a deed that would have major effects for the world as we know it in this puzzling jigsaw of life!

The answers would soon unveil themselves, answers I could have never dreamt of, not even in my wildest dreams.

As more and more passengers got on board the train I became a little anxious, wondering who else would sit next to me – after all, I had another hour's journey to go and let's face it an hour seems like an eternity to an impatient teenager. Surprisingly the seat next to me remained empty and the train set away, huffing and puffing, keen to let the open countryside know it was passing by.

The next hour was spent munching on a picnic of sweets ranging from good old fashioned menthol cough sweets to my favourite aniseed balls. The old lady sat peering through her tiny round spectacles as she continued embroidering a piece of cloth. Every once in a while she would glance up, smile and then look straight back down, eager to complete her craft. The train pulled into the station and I gathered my belongings to alight the train. As I stepped off there in front of me was a familiar object, a satin handkerchief, like the one which had belonged to the kind gentleman who had returned my favourite pen to me on the train earlier. I picked it up, yes it was his, it had the same initials BJR on it. I looked around to see if I could see him but the station was busy with passengers getting on and off the train and their families were all crowded around to say hello or farewell. Unfortunately I could not return the favour, so I crumpled it up and put it in my backpack bag.

Stepping on to the platform I spotted Pops, all smiles and waving so frantically the passengers on an aeroplane could not fail to see him. Greeting him I could almost smell the warmth and comforting aroma of Nan's freshly baked bread.

"Hello, my little angel, broth tonight and some of Nan's special dough bread made just for you when we get home. I bet you're scranny," said Pops in his wonderful broad Northumbrian accent.

"Mmm, lovely, I can't wait," I replied enthusiastically. My tummy started to stir, making moans and wailing like a once dormant volcano preparing to awaken.

Stepping into their small but idyllic cottage, I was jumped upon and grasped by my Nan who almost cuddled me to death. A big woman with a big heart. She always made me feel as though I had come home. She had grey hair and the bluest of blue, clear, sparkling eyes. Her skin was flawless, no wrinkles, no blemishes, with pert rosy cheeks; she was untouched by the hands of time. The kitchen was a culinary heaven, smells of warm spices and aromatic odours filled the air. The kitchen benches were full of her home baking. Nan loved to bake, scones, currant buns, rock cakes and a whole host of traditional Northumbrian fayre were produced on a daily basis. If she was not baking for some charity or fundraising event then she was delighting the neighbours, who were always very willing to thankfully accept her kindness. I knew it wouldn't be long before she was stuffing me with all her daily bakes.

"You have lost weight, Cassie," she said and a thought

entered my head: if I stayed here longer than the one week holiday I doubted I would fit into my new jeans, or worse still my ghostly, untanned, white flesh would protrude through the designer rips. Still, it was lovely to feel looked after, taken care of and wanted. Having parents who were divorced and working hard on enjoying their newfound freedom, it was a welcoming change to feel like a priority.

Don't get me wrong, I knew Mum and Dad loved me but they both worked full time and it wasn't easy trying to keep them both happy. A weekend with one, the next weekend with the other. Not just one new home but effectively two. Thankfully they were not horrible about each other, Dad said they had just grown apart and had taken each other for granted. Mum said, "The spark was gone" and no explanation, just simply that, with four simple words she had totally dismissed 20 years of marriage.

Still I was thankful, thankful it had ended like it did, not like all the horror stories my friends would tell me about their estranged parents.

After a relaxing warm bath, I settled in front of the bewitching open fire with a bowl of Nan's hot stew and a delicious chunk of her special bread. As I gazed at the flames I remembered feeling as though life could not get much better than this.

Snuggled up in bed, caressing the fleecy white flannelette blankets to my nose, I curled my knees up high to avoid the thick, coarse tartan scratchy wool blanket that lay on top. Sleep came quickly like a welcome visitor; I soon drifted off.

Chapter Four

The Wishing Bench

I awoke to the sprightly whistling of Pops and outside my window was the distinct sweet smell of tobacco oozing from his pipe. A few minutes later Nan came into my bedroom with a mammoth number of delights on her breakfasting tray.

"Morning, Cassie, here is a hearty breakfast for you. You've a busy day ahead of you, lass, so get stuck in".

Nan stood there with traces of flour on her apron and what looked like smudges of marmalade or jam on her delicate cheek. "Mm, thanks, Nan, my favourite homemade damson and plum jam," I said looking at the tantalising and tasty little pot of preserve on my tray.

"Your Grandad has been awake for hours getting his trowels and all the equipment ready for today. I swear he is more excited than you, a big kid he is," she said, whilst brushing open my thick, green velvet curtains.

"Oh! Yes," I replied enthusiastically not wanting to make it obvious that in fact I had actually forgotten about our plans for today.

Day one's activity was to go metal detecting. Sometimes we would go to the local woods, a farmer's field and other times we would go to the beach. After breakfast I had a quick shower. A very quick shower if that's what you could call it – it was sort of rubber tubes connected to the hot and cold taps and a flat shower head at the end. It was kept above the bath, held on by a simple plastic hook which was stuck to the wall and if it had a kink or twist in the tube the water would not come out properly. The first thing to do was to try and get the water just right otherwise you could shock yourself with a lashing of freezing cold water or equally as harrowing scald yourself with boiling hot water.

After getting dressed I went outside to see what Pops had left out for me to pack in my backpack. A small trowel, a penknife (for special intricate digging) and a small paintbrush ready to dust off the dirt from all those hidden treasures I was about to find. "What's this?" I said to myself, picking up some see-through plastic type gloves. The kind you would use when dyeing your hair so as to not let the chemical touch your skin, pretty ironic seeing you were putting the chemicals directly on your scalp! A worrying thought really. Pops had always made me wear gloves and Pops always did too. I guess because he suffered from some skin allergy, I was never really sure what it was but I remember he always wore them. I remember the time we were walking and I saw a penny lying on the ground. "Look, Pops," I shouted, "see a penny pick it ..." and before I could get the words out of my mouth he shouted, "NO! Don't touch it, you don't know where it's been, filthy thing, all the germs on it". I remembering feeling shocked. I had never heard Pops shout before and all because I was going to pick up a penny! Maybe he was getting some odd habits as he got older or maybe like I learned in year 11 Physiology he maybe, I think it was one in five men, had some form of OCD (Obsessive Compulsive Disorder). I now know none of those ideas were right, he was doing what grandfathers do best... he was PROTECTING me.

The only thing left to pack was my scrumptious packed lunch Nan had put up for me and I was ready for an adventure.

You could smell the relentless stench of the seaweed tainting and stinging our nostrils long before we reached the beach. A procession of quick sneezes and I knew we had arrived.

CHAPTER FOUR

It was a mild but very pleasant day, warm enough just to wear a tee shirt and I was pleased it was not too hot. I didn't really do 'hot'. With blonde hair and very pale skin and freckles I was the perfect example of an English rose.

It all sounds very idyllic but in fact what it really meant in reality was that I would literally frazzle in the summer sun. Thankfully living in the north of the country sunshine was something we didn't see much of except on those rare boiling hot summer's days when the sun decided to pay us special attention.

Today was perfect weather for metal detecting I told myself because believe it or not you could get quite hot and sweaty when digging frantically after every buzz. Each time I heard that elusive buzz my heart would miss a beat and I would consciously stop breathing. In utter silence I would listen, my ears straining to block out every other noise, every other sound just so I could listen to that all important buzz. I would gush and feel a sudden sense of excitement, together with a strange burst of energy as I thought about the amazing possibilities that lay ahead.

I had never really found anything of any importance or value. A two pence piece, the metal ring pull from an old can or my biggest item yet, an old milk churn lid which I found six inches beneath water in a stream.

It was not long before we began to march up and

down the beach, making imprints in the soft golden sand as we moved slowly so as not to miss an inch. Gently swaying the metal detector back and forth, hovering it just above the sand, like a rattlesnake waiting to attack its unsuspecting prey. After a couple of buzzes here and there but no great finds it was time to stop and have a bite to eat and a drink.

Way up high in the distance, I could see at the very top of a grassed over mound was an old wooden bench seat.

"Look, Pops," I said pointing to the bench. "Can we go up there and sit for a bit? The view from there would be spectacular I bet?"

"It sure is, Cassie, that is the old 'Wishing bench'," said Pops, nodding his head in agreement.

"Wishing bench?" I said, intrigued by what he was on about.

"Yes," he said, smiling with a very curious glint in his sparkling blue eyes. "It is said that if you are a good soul and are pure of heart during certain times in your life, probably when you least expect it and when someone really needs it, you can sit on that seat and make a wish and it will come true but perhaps not in the way you imagined."

"Wow, really?" I gasped, imagining all the different

things I would wish for. My mind was going into overdrive, a bit like if you had just found out you had won the lottery and you were thinking about all the different things you could buy. I started thinking about who I would like to help – definitely Nan and Pops, a nice big house, a lovely holiday and maybe a top of the range metal detector for Pops. Then there would be my mum and dad, my cousins and my friends. Then I realised it, suddenly it came to me, there wasn't anything I really wanted. I had everything that really mattered to me, my family... how lucky I was. Looking at Pops and his smiling, cheerful face, I noticed the lines on his forehead and eyes. I hadn't really noticed them before, he was just Pops with salt and pepper grey hair, always combed in a stylish quiff and a style all of his own. He somehow looked a little shorter, a little older too. Maybe there was one thing I could wish for? Yes that's it, I would climb the mound, sit on the seat and make my wish.

"I wish Nan and Pops would never grow older and they would never leave me." If only wishes did come true, I sighed.

Pops and I climbed the mound and sat down, ready to eat our delicious packed lunch. Putting my hand in my backpack it felt like I was playing lucky dip, only this time I knew I would not be disappointed.

"Yummy," I squealed in delight. "A currant bun, my favourite."

"Yes, Nan put in extra currants for you too," said Pops as he munched through the mini feast. The view from the mound was really stunning. I could see the old lighthouse in the distance, standing like a beacon of hope, sturdy and proud as the reckless waves battered its stem. Looking out towards the sea I noticed how visible the sharp, rugged rocks had become. The sea was way out and all the landscape had gone through a miraculous change. Rocks of all different sizes and shapes grazed the coastline like cattle on a deserted barren field. A rainbow danced above in the clear blue sky, vivid colours of indigo and green splashed the horizon with a graceful pose. Whenever I saw a rainbow I always looked to see if I could see its beginning and end.

"A pot of gold," murmuring my thoughts out loud.

"What's that, my petal?" said Pops in a curious manner.

"The rainbow, Pops, they say there is a pot of gold at the end of every rainbow," I replied.

"I see," said Pops. "Well I'm not sure about a pot of gold but that looks like a small cave just where the rainbow ends."

Just as I stood up to get a better look my backpack

fell behind the seat and a strange feeling came over me. I went behind the seat to pick it up. Bending on my knees I noticed some writing etched into the wooden seat. R...E, M I think another E M B E and finally an R. REMEMBER followed what looked like a stick drawing of a helicopter or winged bug or swirly shape or something like that.

Remember? Remember what? Remember a bug? What a strange thing to write on a seat. Not like the usual graffiti you would normally see. No 'Peter loves Clare' scraped into a huge heart, no graffiti artist's tag, just the word remember and a funny drawing. How strange but I guess it made sense to someone.

Picking up my bag I sat back on the wooden seat. I wondered who had carved the word, who had sat on the seat before me, all those people throughout time probably before I was born, all those people making wishes.

"Pops, how old do you think this bench is?"

Pops shook his head. "Oh, Cassie, this bench has been here as long as I can remember, ever since I was a young boy. I believe it was put here by an inventor, some famous man who loved holidaying here in Brew and put this seat here so people for years to come could sit up here on the mound and admire the beautiful scenery. It's very special," he said, looking at me in a strange and serious way. "Did I ever tell you, this is the exact spot where I asked your Nan to marry me?"

Pops then went on to tell me how he and Nan had been for a walk along the same path as we were on today. How they had walked up the grassy mound and watched the sunset over the sea then just before the last rays of daylight passed he got down on one knee and proposed. "I got my wish on that day," he said. "She said yes and my dreams all came true, first your dad and then the most precious gift of all ...you."

Chapter Five

The Secret Cave

Gathering our possessions together we climbed down the mound, paying extra attention and being careful not to slip as there was a lot of unkempt weeds and nettles lining our path. Having been stung at an early age by a nettle the memory of the pain had stayed with me. Thank god for dock leaves, however! Pops had very quickly plucked such a leaf and rubbed its miraculous sap on my injured knee. How instantly the pain had subsided and although I kept crying all the way home the powers of the leaf had made a lasting impression on me.

As we walked along the beach I was eager to explore the secret cave. It was almost impossible to see; in fact if it had not been for the rainbow acting as a guide it could have remained hidden forever. Pops and I began to walk over to the edge of the water, our shoes becoming damp by the salty sea water. We stopped and peered over.

"It doesn't seem that deep, Pops. Do you think we could go and have a look inside?" I asked, desperate for his agreement.

"Not today, Cassie," he replied, "enough secrets for one day."

"Secrets?" I asked to no reply.

Nan was at the cottage keen to find out if we had discovered any treasures, smiling and giggling as she watched a popular tea time game show on TV.

I kicked off my shoes and sat on the big comfy armchair. Looking around the lounge I seemed to take more notice of the furnishings than usual. On one wall was a set of three display cabinets. This was where Pops kept his 'antiquities' or really old weird things of not much value in my opinion.

Amongst them were a broken medieval spur, a stone with some strange carvings on it and an old clay pipe. I noticed today, for the first time, each of the cabinets were locked and there were no keys protruding from the locks. If I was a burglar those things would be the last things I would take, I thought, but still the fact that the cases were locked had me wondering why.

I remember as a young girl I once asked to try on an old set of beads from the case; they were Egyptian Faience beads supposedly found in Egyptian burial sites. Pops point blankly refused, only saying, "You must never touch anything in those cases, Cassie, never TOUCH anything."

As I looked in one of the cases drawn on an old piece of parchment type paper was a familiar symbol and it seemed to shout out at me. Where had I seen it before? Racking my brain I just couldn't think but it looked so familiar.

That night I slept like a dog; it must have been all that fresh sea air and long walks. Pops and Nan were going into the next village today. They had asked if I wanted to go with them but to be honest I fancied just chilling, doing my own thing and hanging about. After Nan had fussed about me and then showed what she had made me for lunch, she and Pops headed out.

I spent the next hour snap chatting Phoebe, checking out my mate's statuses on Facebook whilst trying to look at my revision notes for the forthcoming exams. I looked out of the window. It looked like such a nice day, far too nice to be stuck in, that was for sure. I went to get a drink from the fridge and noticed the bottle of coca cola I had put in yesterday, unopened.

So much for taking that chance, I thought to myself, what happened to my letter in the bottle?

"That's it," I said excitedly out loud. I jumped up and

put my shoes on, packed my bag with a few of Nan's delicious cooked treats and headed off to finish my mission.

I decided where best to write my letter but on the 'Wishing bench', so I made my way up the mound.

Sitting on the seat I took out my notebook and empty plastic bottle and prepared to write the letter, which, although I didn't realise it at the time, would help save my life!

Dear Finder,

Hi my name is Cassie and I am 16 years old. The year is 2017 and I am sending this letter in the bottle from the village of Brew in England.

I'm writing this letter in the hope that it will bring adventure, fortune and luck. I am ready for whatever fate has to offer, ready to take a chance and ready to meet my destiny.

Cassie x

Taking my shoes off I carefully made my way along the beach, trying to avoid stepping on the sharp broken shells and rough pebbles. Trying to balance on the green slippery moss-covered rock pools, I grimaced. "Ouch, Ow, ahhh," I screeched as my foot touched the freezing cold water and my little piggy toe scraped along a rough edge.

Looking out to sea I waited for the next visit by the all-encompassing, sweeping wave. Thrusting the bottle as far as I could throw, I watched as my dreams were slowly washed away into the horizon.

I stood for a moment and felt accomplished. It wasn't just the bottle that had been washed away, so had all my self-doubt and I felt like me, the old me.

I was just about to start walking back when something got my attention from the corner of my eye and as I turned, there it was almost inviting me in… The cave.

As I reached the entrance I shuddered and felt a slight chill in the air. Stepping inside I was surprised at how dim and cold it was. A scary thought entered my head; I hoped there were no inhabitants, no bats.

An eerie feeling came over me and a sudden noise made me jump in fright. As I turned around I saw an ugly seagull pottering around searching for something in the cave. Its yellow beak had a bright red mark on it which made it look quite menacing. "Ugly bird," I whispered.

The air smelt cold, forgotten and unwanted. There was nothing in the cave, no markings on the walls, just sand, seaweed and pebbles lining the floor. It was pretty dark and not at all as inviting as it first appeared.

A bee whizzed by and the buzz echoed around the walls of the cave, like a hymn being sang in an old monastery; it filled the air. I hated bees and started to jump and dance, kicking the damp sand off my feet; I looked down. There in the crumbs beneath my toes lay a smooth but misshapen glistening object. I slowly started to scrape away the damp sand with my fingertips, watching as I created little pyramids. With each stroke my heart seemed to stop beating so as not to make a noise, cause a distraction.

I felt my eyes widen in anticipation, not wanting to miss a second of the uncovering of my discovery.

"Wow, look at this," I said out loud as I gently uncovered what looked like to be a very delicate, old metal pin in the shape of an aeroplane. Rich yellowy and golden in colour almost like burnt gold, it was about the size of a two pence piece. It was very uneven in its thickness and seemed poorly made but it glistened and had kept its shape after years of being at the mercy of the sea and elements. I gently rubbed it against my t shirt in an attempt to restore it to its former glory. Looking closely I could see a small emblem engraved on the wing, like a swirl; something about the symbol was familiar.

There in my small, delicate, shaky hand lay a small pin, the type you would see on the lapels of those old men who were keen aircraft enthusiasts. I would often see them on tweed jackets worn by men the same age as Pops. Sometimes they would be in the shape of cars, sometimes trains, and all sorts really; still it was a cool find and I couldn't wait to show Pops.

I gazed at the interesting pin for what seemed to be an eternity then I carefully took a tissue from my jeans pocket and wrapped it up tight inside. Putting it back deep inside my pocket to rest, I started to make my way out of the cave.

As I walked a step closer to the entrance I felt as though I was floating, almost gliding feeling, swept away by the total encounter. Suddenly a bright light shone into the cave and I was quickly and abruptly brought back down to earth.

A fierce and all-encompassing heat raged throughout my body. The air had turned warm and my lips felt dry. Stepping out of the cave my eyes smarted as I put my hand up to cover and protect them from the glaring sunlight.

"It's turned out to be a scorching hot day," I thought. "Wish I had brought my sunglasses."

Once my eyes had become adjusted to the powerful

sunlight I began to fixate on my surroundings. The shoreline looked completely different; the sea even looked a different colour. Blues, purples and all shades of green swished and swashed in each gallant wave. The rocks had lost their green moss and looked patchy, a little barren and dry. There was different greenery, different to that in Brew. As I gazed down towards the sand I stood in utter confusion. In disbelief. The sand was no longer golden, it was dirty, almost black. In fact it did not even look like sand at all, more like a blanket of crushed charcoal, like the charcoal stems I sometimes used in art. I reached down and grabbed a handful. It was not soft or delicate as it ran through my fingers; it was sharp and gritty, like crushed shells and crushed pebbles.

"What's happened? Where am I?" I whispered, scared to break the silence, scared to make it reality. I looked around scouring my surroundings, looking for a familiar feature.

The mound was gone. The old church on the cliff edge was gone. The wishing bench was gone. I WAS GONE... But to where?

As I took a step further I grimaced as the black sand beneath me burned and scalded my naked feet. I stood hopping from one foot onto the other like some crazy frog. I began to tip toe through the pools of water and I was comforted by how warm and refreshing it was. I reached the edge of the cave entrance. I stood looking, knowing something was not right. "Where am I and more importantly how can I get back home?" The words escaped my lips as I stood contemplating my predicament.

Chapter Six

Meeting Barnes

A shriek and a scream suddenly made me come out of my confusion. Looking towards the sea I could see a small child jumping up and down, waving their hands violently in despair. I looked around and no one else was visible, there was no one on the beach, just the child and me at the entrance to the cave. I started to walk towards her and as I grew closer I could see it was a young girl. She was jumping in and out of the sea and screaming, "Help me, help me!" Her high pitched screams bellowed in the warm air and I began to run. There was something being swallowed and tossed by the waves far in the distance.

"My brother, my brother Barney, he is out there, he can't get back, please help us!" The young girl managed to get the broken words out as she struggled to catch her breath, the tears streaming down her pale little cheeks.

She was dressed in some old fashioned kind of costume, completely covered up and the material was ghastly, a horrible kaki brown, awful.

I looked towards the sea again, clenching my fist together to create a makeshift telescope. Looking through my own pinhole camera, I captured first an arm then a bare leg being flung about and engulfed by the treacherous sea.

I'm not sure where I got my strength that day, my bravery and my determination. All I know is that nothing else mattered except that poor boy and that I had to save him.

Throwing down my bag and my jacket, I quickly took off my jeans and top; luckily I had my bathing suit underneath in case I had fancied trying to get a bit of a tan.

I jumped into the sea and found myself battling each wave with every ounce of me. I was a strong swimmer and was first in my junior class to get all my swimming badges, going on to take my lifeguard training at our local baths.

But this was real and no amount of training or pretend role play can prepare you for the stark reality of being responsible for the life or death of another human being.

The waves kept coming fast and the current was deceitful, trying to swamp my body and take me far out with it. I could still faintly hear the young girl's desperate scream as I fought the sea and then all of a sudden I could see the boy, he was in arm's reach of me.

"Hold my neck, put your arm around my neck, keep a hold and swim with me," I gurgled to the boy.

His eyes were all glazed and bloodshot, his face pale and had been cut by a rock or some equally hidden danger in the sea. His arms and shoulders were bleeding too. I'm not sure if he understood what I was saying, his eyes kept rolling to the back of his head and his mouth kept spewing out the sea. I really didn't think he was going to make it and I was scared.

I managed to swim with him wrapped around me like an old rag doll until I dropped him free on to the shore. The young girl was distraught as he lay there not moving, not breathing.

"Keep clear, I can do this," I said as I urged the young girl to clear the way.

I put all my life saving knowledge into practice, turned him on his side and as he started to breathe again I watched as the salty water was expelled from his body. It was not time for Poseidon to take him. At least not today.

The boy kept spurting at the mouth and his lips started to regain some colour other than the blueish grey shade they were when he was released by the sea. His face seemed less sallow and although he had nasty gashes and trickles of blood running down his cheeks he had started to look more like a boy and not like a lifeless, porcelain faced old raggedy puppet. I bent down into my bag and looked for something to wipe away the blood on his face; the first thing I touched was the silk handkerchief I had found. Taking it from my bag I gently wiped his forehead.

"You will be fine, just take it easy, you've been through a terrible ordeal," I reassured the boy. I looked and smiled at his young sister, who immediately came over to me and put her arms around me, embracing me.

"Thank you, thank you so much. Father has told Barnes not to swim out so far; he never listens! I think it's because he has something to prove!" The young girl started to shout uncontrollably at her older brother.

Barnes started to sit up, leaning on his shaky hand and struggling to regain some composure. He shook his head and his mop of floppy sandy blonde hair fell on to his face covering his obvious embarrassment. He looked around my age although it was hard to tell but one thing was for sure: he had absolutely no taste in clothes, I mean where had he got those shorts he was wearing from? It had to be a dare!

He slowly looked up at me through the protection of his floppy fringe, his painful eyes still recovering from the sharp sting of the sea salted water.

"I really don't know how to thank you, you have saved my life. My leg went into cramp and I just lost it." He then turned his attentions. "I am sorry," he said, looking over to his poor, distraught younger sister.

The poor little girl released her tight grip of me and almost fell on her older brother. I just sat and took a deep breath, trying to comprehend everything that had just happened.

As Barnes and his sister stood up, I too managed to stand, albeit a bit shaky. I felt my legs were going to cave in underneath me, I was exhausted.

Barnes held out his hand to shake mine. I was a bit taken aback – what 16 year old does that? I felt out of my comfort zone, I was not a touchy, feely kind of person except with dogs and I liked my own space. Still I did not want to appear rude so I had my first ever handshake that day and I am still unsure whether I did it right.

"Hi, my name is Cassie, pleased to meet you," I greeted him.

"This is my sister Annie," he said, looking at the little waif, dishevelled blonde girl next to him.

Annie was so petite, with long blonde hair and impish features. She was holding her brother's hand and started to swing it like young children do. I would have loved a sister, or a brother – being the only child wasn't much fun growing up. I had my cousins David and Vanessa and Paul who were from my aunts, my mum's two sisters. We all used to meet on a Sunday at my other Nan's house and have Sunday lunch together and my Nan would babysit us all as our parents would be at work. We would all get bathed at Nan's and my Nan would plait my hair whilst it was wet ready for school in the morning so when I took them out I would have an abundance of crazy curls. My younger cousin Vanessa would cry behind the sofa – having very short hair she felt left out. My cousin David, although only a year younger than me, was very shy and quiet. He would just look on, playing with his 'Sweep', a soft, grey cuddly dog he used to carry everywhere. The youngest, Paul, would be joking about winding up everyone. It was nice to think about happier times with my cousins. I guess we were all more like brothers and sisters but as we all grew older the time we spent together faded and all I had left was my memories.

"Would you like to come to tea with us?" asked Annie, looking up at me with big doe eyes. "Mother and Father will not mind, especially when I tell them how you saved

Barney's life."

"No you mustn't," interrupted Barney. "I don't mean don't come for tea, I just mean please don't tell my parents what happened today." His anxious tone and desperate plea made me nod in agreement – after all where else had I got to go, in fact where exactly was I?

I bent down and lifted up my top and jeans from the damp sand, shaking them off before I put them back on.

Falling from my jeans pocket was the little aeroplane pin badge dropping out from the paper tissue I had wrapped it in earlier.

Barney bent down and picked it up, staring at it as though he had just seen a long lost treasure. "Where did you get this?" he asked, holding out the pin.

"I found it over there in that cave, just before I came out and heard your sister screaming. Why?" I asked, puzzled by his behaviour.

"It's mine – at least I think it is, I lost it here last summer when we were on holiday last year. I searched everywhere for it but couldn't find it. I was given it by a pilot, a patient of my father's who is more of a family friend now."

"Patient?" I asked curious to learn more.

"Yes, my father is a doctor and he was a patient of my father before my father became ill."

"Oh I'm sorry your dad is ill," I said, genuinely interested to find out more.

"Don't be. I've always known him to be the way he is, he contracted polio when I was about six. It affected him quite badly at first but he doesn't let it stop him; although he is crippled, he gets about fine on his metal framed tricycle."

"Tricycle?" I started to picture the little three wheeled cycles the kids in our street would play on, but I couldn't imagine an adult on one, let alone a doctor! He must be some crazy eccentric! I thought to myself. "Doesn't he use one of those super charged electrical scooters or chairs?" I asked, curious for his reply.

"I have no idea what you mean, I have never seen one," he replied.

"You have never seen one? Where do you live?" I asked, not quite believing him "You see loads of old and disabled people on them nowadays. On the pavements, in shops, down the high street, everywhere."

"Well we moved to number 241 New Cross Road in London in 1889 when I was two and I can honestly say I've never seen the kind of contraption you are on about."

I looked at him, waiting for a small grin, a glint in his eyes to show me he was trying to have some kind of stupid joke with me but there was nothing. His face, although it was straight, looked a little intrigued as he tried to picture the 'contraption' I was on about.

"1889," I said again just in case the sea water had damaged my hearing.

"Yes in 1889, although I go to school at Christ's Hospital in Horsham – it was founded in 1552. My brother John and I were nominated to take an entrance exam for a scholarship by Colonel Newcome and we both got in, thankfully – it meant Father does not have to pay."

"Yes and Barnes came 7th out of 110 boys and got awarded a plaque too," said Annie excited and so very proud of her older brother.

"1889," I said under my breath. I knew I was no longer in Brew when I came out of the cave but to learn I was not even in the same year was just totally too much to believe.

Barnes was still standing holding the aeroplane badge in his hand. "I'm so thankful I met you today, Cassie, firstly you save my life and then return to me a much loved trinket I thought I had lost forever." He put it deep into his wet shorts pocket.

The walk along the shore was full of questions and guarded answers by myself – let's face it I couldn't actually say, "Well I'm from the future and the reality is you will have both been dead a long time in my world!" I had to think fast to not appear like a lunatic if that's the right word because I am sure I watched some documentary in citizenship at school how in the 1900s they would put people in asylums and torture them! On top of that Barnes's dad was a doctor so he could probably get me sent to one as easy as booking a table at your favourite restaurant for lunch. No way! I had to be careful what I would say if I was ever going to survive in the past.

I made up a story. I too was on holiday with a great uncle who was far too busy to be saddled with a 16 year old girl, so I was left to my own devices. They were curious about my strange clothes, my jeans in particular because it was unusual to see a young lady in trousers. I made some excuse that it was common play clothes where I came from in Brew, near the Scottish borders. As soon as I mentioned Scotland to them it all made sense because everyone north of London were a little barbaric and seemed a little 'backward and colloquial' for the times. After all the ladies in London were amongst if not the most fashionable in the modern world. An argument I was very happy on this occasion to concede.

"See over there," said Barnes, pointing to what looked like a huge shipyard in the distance. That's where they work on naval destroyers, here in Cowes." His eyes lit up as he became animated. "I want to be an engineer and work there one day."

"Cowes," I said whispering to myself; so that's where I was.

"Barnes and John are always making things at home," said little Annie, keen to enter into the conversation. "They have their own workshop at home and Father lets them make things. I have lots of paper aeroplanes and other creations."

"John?" I asked.

"Yes he is our brother too, but unlike Barnes he never gets into trouble like today!" she said, sure to not let her brother forget his misadventures of the day.

It wasn't long before we got to a small cottage not far from the beach itself.

Inside was like walking into a museum. It reminded me of when I visited the museum in York which had different exhibitions looking at life in England throughout the ages. Only this was no museum reliving history, I had found myself living the history and I had no way out.

"Annie, take Cassie into the drawing room, make her comfortable please," said Barnes as he left us and went upstairs to change clothes and clean his wounds.

Barnes's mother and father were not in but the young housemaid looked after us by making us tea in the small drawing room. We had tea in blue and white floral china teacups. The tea was served on similar decorated saucers which helped me balance the delicate cup; still slightly shaking I didn't want to drop it. There was a selection of small sandwiches and what looked like a malted tea loaf thinly sliced on the china platter in front of us.

The sun had soon dried my long blonde hair and I was left with curls and wisps decorating my shoulder line. I looked into my bag to pull out my small mirror, and was thankful to discover I did not look as terrible as I actually felt.

I looked around the furnishings. There were lots of tapestry type pictures framed on the wall, on the mantelpiece there were different references to the seaside, conch shells and those shells that looked like they were made from mother of pearl in the shape of a trumpet.

Barnes entered the room and looked regenerated and recovered from his near death experience. His hair was brushed to the side and he smiled as he sat with Annie and me.

Over our 'high tea' Barnes and his sister told me lots of stories about the fun time they had each year on holiday, I tried to look interested and engage in conversation but my mind kept drifting back to Brew. How was I going to get home, how had I ended up here? How had I gone back in time? And what would poor Nan and Pops be thinking?

A thought entered my head and I gasped; I would be a missing person! My face would no doubt be splattered all over social media and everyone would know.

"I have to get back home," I said out loud, sounding quite desperate.

"Oh do you have to?" said Annie, relishing having some female company instead of her brothers.

"Would your uncle really mind if you stayed with me tonight?" she said, almost begging me to meet her request.

It was then reality started to set in and I realised, actually I had nowhere to go, nowhere to sleep, I was alone and I felt terrified.

"I am sure he would not mind," I said eager to take her up on her offer. "I will pop back to leave a message for him." I bent into my bag and pulled out my favourite pen and my notebook. As I opened the book and started to write a fabricated letter to my fake uncle I noticed the indentations on the paper from the letter I had only written a few hours earlier but in reality I had not even written! The letter I had written and posted in my bottle was written in 2017 and that was in more than a hundred years' time.

I thought about what I had wished for, Adventure, ready to take a chance and fulfil my destiny.

Was that it? Was that why I had ended up here? It must have been the Wishing bench, it was real and it had granted me my wish. Although when I wrote the letter I must admit this was definitely not what I had expected would happen to me. So if it had got me here, maybe that was it! Maybe I had to find another magic bench and write another letter. As I thought about it I felt myself shaking my head, I knew it just wasn't going to happen.

"What is your address?" I asked trying to convince the pair that I was indeed writing a real letter.

I quickly scribbled a note basically saying I would be staying at 'The seafarers lodge' with Barnes and Annie Wallis and I would return the following day.

"I will just pop out and take this back to my cottage," I said, quickly getting up, keen on leaving by myself after all. I didn't want them to follow me.

"Would you like us to accompany you, Cassie?" asked Barnes, gallant and polite as ever.

"It's fine, thank you, I won't be too long, I may have to spend a little time with my uncle if he is home and he is a very private person, quite shy, never married." I kept adding on lots of excuses as to why my uncle would not want to meet them and why it was best I went back myself.

They walked me to the front door and waved as I walked down the street.

"See you soon." I heard the faint cry of young Annie echoing in the air.

As I wandered down a small lane I kept looking out for different features on the street, things that I could remember to enable me to get back. The last thing I wanted was to get lost as well as everything else. I saw the beach very quickly and I made my way to the start of my adventure. As I was getting nearer a strange feeling came over me, the kind of eerie feeling that you are being followed. I tried to tactfully look over my shoulder, half expecting to see young Annie following in my footsteps.

I stood for a second until I could build up the confidence to look behind. I turned abruptly but there was no one there, although I thought I saw a quick glimpse of someone wearing a long coat dart around the corner but I soon dismissed it and put it down to my nerves. I sat for a while on the shingle beach, looking over to where the entrance to the cave was. Would it be worthwhile trying to go back into the cave and seeing if I could get back home? I decided it would but not today: the cruel tide was in and anyway I really felt a sense of responsibility and could not let poor Annie down by just disappearing without saying goodbye.

I was just about to get up and head back to Seafarers Cottage when I had that feeling someone was watching me again, I looked behind me and there was no one suspicious around. A few children were on the beach with what I assumed could be their nanny, at least that is what I thought, very Nanny McPhee type. The young girl had a long skirt right down to her ankles and some little black type boots. She wore a type of hooded cape and her hair was tied back into a formal bun. Yeah, definitely a nanny.

As I watched the children play my eye was distracted by a shapely, vague figure standing up high on the promenade. I don't know what it was that made me notice it but I had an unnerving feeling about it. I think it looked like a man; I could not tell for sure as he was too far away. He was by himself and was just standing there, watching. Not another soul was on the promenade. Maybe he was the children's father, I said to myself, trying to dismiss my tense, disturbing, gut feeling. Then I started wondering if he was their father, where was their mother? As I picked up my bag and started walking towards the promenade, the ghostly figure abruptly walked away and within seconds had disappeared, completely out of view. "Well he obviously wasn't their dad," I spoke out loud, so who was he? As I walked past where the stranger had stood I looked down and saw the outline of that all too familiar shape drawn on the loose, dirty sand which had been blown on to the white stone. I bent down, looking down at it... where had I seen it before? It looked like it had wings or blades, I racked my brain trying to recall why it looked familiar but I just couldn't remember. Had the stranger drawn it? Or was it nothing, was it even a shape? Or was just my mind playing games with me? I shook my head and in doing so shook off all thought of it and the stranger.

I soon found myself at the cottage with a warm and excited greeting from Annie. Barnes and his brother John were working on their 'Invention' in their bedroom. Their parents had been home and then had left again having to cut their holiday short to deal with urgent business back home. The Wallis children were left in the good hands of the maid who seemed on occasion to double up as their nanny.

"Let's go and see the boys," said Annie, gripping my hand and dragging me into a room at the back of the cottage. Before we opened the door I could hear the two boys discussing their new project.

"Hi Cassie," said Barnes, "this is our brother John." I smiled at the boy next to him as he smiled back and then continued to scribble notes on the sketches in front of him.

The boys started to tell me all about how they were keen inventors and how they were working on a 'super aeroplane'. Annie and I left them to it and spent the rest of the evening talking until we both drifted off into a very deep sleep.

Chapter Seven

The Symbol

Morning came and it was another day, a whole 24 hours I would have been 'missing'. I needed to get home, I needed to revisit my steps and go back to the cave, and I needed to try.

I went into the bathroom and having slept in my bathing costume, I put the previous day's clothes on. I heard the maid call from the parlour room, "breakfast", then a scuttle of running feet. I soon joined them and enjoyed a fine selection of malted bread and preserves.

"We are going down to the beach this morning, Cassie, John and I want to try out our ideas!" said Barnes enthusiastically. "Are you joining us?"

"Yes absolutely, I sure am," I said emphatically, in fact it was the one thing, the only thing that I was sure about.

The boys and Annie went and collected their things

and we all left together. As we approached the promenade my mind thought back to yesterday and the stranger, the man who had been standing looking out towards the sea.

Walking onto the dark shingle beach the boys threw down their backpacks and took out what looked like model aeroplanes. I thought about the boys back home at school, about Austin. There is no way they would be seen dead 'playing with' model planes! How things had changed. I wondered what Barnes and his brother would think about 'the Xbox' or 'PlayStation'; they wouldn't believe it.

As the boys started to fly their planes and measure the distances they flew, Barnes began to scribble down mathematical equations and formulas. I watched for a bit; I was quite impressed how intelligent they seemed to be, if not a bit boring.

My attention turned to young Annie standing throwing pebbles into the water and watching as they sunk into the deep sea.

"What you need to do, Annie, is find flat stones, something like this," I said, showing Annie a flat, smooth, polished stone I had picked up from the shore.

"Watch me," I told her as I threw the stone.

My grandad, Pops, had shown me when I was a young child how to throw stones into the sea and how to make them go really far and not sink, making them skim over the waves and bounce.

The trick was, firstly, to pick an aerodynamic stone that was smooth and symmetrical in shape. Then it was how you threw it, standing legs apart and your shoulder adjacent to the sea; you had to throw it so it glided. Gracefully kissing the waves as it bounced from one to another until it met its final destination.

I threw one, then two as Annie started to jump up and down with excitement. "Wow, look at how far it's gone!" she said, impressed with my skimming skills.

Barnes hearing all the commotion came over and watched, also impressed with me. He soon started to sketch and scribble as he asked me to keep throwing them. Had he really never seen anyone skim a stone before? I guess not; I suppose nothing surprised me anymore.

He started to baffle me with all this physics stuff telling me the scientific reason why the stone was travelling so far. Unfortunately I hated science; it just wasn't my thing. I preferred English and drama so I started, not intentionally, switching off. I thought about this kid in class Jenson; he was actually a cool kid despite being a bit of a swot at science. He was really tall with dark hair and bright blue eyes and was a hit with the girls in year 11 and even the 6th formers from what I had heard. He had won some prize from one of the local pharmaceutical companies for an idea he had submitted in a competition. I bet he would be able to tell Barnes straight away the scientific equation for the 'stone skim'. I suddenly felt quite useless, I mean here I was from the future and what use was I? What could I actually tell them about? What invention or great discovery? Even if there was something I very much doubt I could tell them how to make it.

"Let me try," said an eager Barnes, picking up a stone from the beach and examining it for its precise circumference and aerodynamic ability.

His attempts failed miserably and he gave up, choosing to look at his scribbled sketches.

Annie was running up and down the beach collecting stones, John was still enjoying flying his handmade plane and Barnes decided to sit with me.

I was looking over to the cave and I could feel tears filling my eyes. I missed home, my grandparents, my friends; I was scared. What if I was stuck here forever? I couldn't keep pretending I was staying with an uncle. When the Wallis family's holiday was over they would go home and then what would happen to me?

"What's wrong?" said Barnes. He was a very astute and intelligent young man and he knew there was something wrong.

I needed a friend, a confidant. I looked at him and I was just about to start spilling the truth, all my incredible and unbelievable secrets, when I put my hand in my bag to search for a tissue, handkerchief.

My fingers searched in the darkness of the bag and out came the handkerchief, the one I had used on Barnes's cut, the one that belonged to that kind gentleman on the train.

Bloodstained – I quickly tossed it on the beach, a natural instinct when you see blood, let alone someone else's!

As it floated down and spread out next to me the initials were revealed as was the motif. B, J, and R and there it was... THE symbol, THE drawing, THE shape. The exact same shape that had been drawn by the stranger on the sand on the promenade. My mind thought back and I remembered the feeling when I first met him. Something wasn't right, and then I remembered when I saw someone with a long coat dart around a corner the other day. A long camel covered coat. The stranger, the man standing watching me on the beach. It was him.

I picked up the handkerchief and put it in my bag.

"What's wrong, Cassie? I'm really concerned about you," said Barnes, watching my despair.

I needed to tell someone, I needed help and someone I could trust but not here, not now, not on the beach with Annie and John around.

"Later, Barnes, I will tell you later when we are alone," I replied.

Barnes just nodded, took my hand in both of his to comfort me and smiled, not wanting to pry any further.

"I'm getting hungry," said John. I think that was one of the only times I had heard him speak.

We all headed back to the cottage and as I walked I found myself looking at the ground for signs.

We all had lunch at the cottage and John went into his room to repair his plane which had been put through its paces earlier, crashing on the beach.

Annie had been asking the maid to help her with a huge embroidered tapestry blanket she was making and eventually the maid agreed, if nothing else to keep her quiet.

Barnes looked at me. "Would you like to talk now?" he said in a kind and calm voice.

"I want to tell you, tell you everything but I am afraid you will think I am crazy, I still cannot believe it myself," I replied nervously.

I sat and told him without even stopping for breath, how I had been in Brew, writing a letter, going into the cave, turning up here and about how I thought a man from my time was here too, following me. It sounded completely barking mad. Totally crazy. So there it was, there I was just waiting for him to offer to tell his father, which would actually mean me getting put into an asylum for the insane and deluded.

But instead he looked at me, not laughing or in disbelief.

"I believe you. From the first moment we met I knew you were different and I do not mean being a Northerner, I'm not that small minded. No one, not even our northern cousins, have clothes like you and the pen you had the other day, I have never seen anything like it."

A huge sense of relief came over me, like a huge weight had lifted from my mind. I started to cry uncontrollably, I just let it all go and poor Barnes had to pick up the pieces and comfort me.

"It will be fine, Cassie, I will help you, we will find a way to get you home and until then do not worry, you can stay with us. I will help you, you are not alone," said Barnes, reassuring me.

I was lucky, out of all the people in the world to have found someone like him, a true friend.

I went to the bathroom to wash my tear stained face and make myself look presentable. I did not want Annie,

John or the maid to see I had been crying.

I decided I needed a little alone time, my head was pounding with crying and I had a splitting headache. I went to Annie's room and lay down on the bed. I must have drifted off to sleep and I woke up with the strong sunbeams shining into the room. I stood up and walked over to the window. Moving the curtain to one side I looked out of the window onto the street below.

Then I saw him standing on the corner of the street; it was him, the stranger.

I quickly ran down the stairs, hearing the boys and Annie in different rooms as I passed. Opening the heavy cottage door, I ran onto the street. I looked from left to right but I couldn't see him; I ran across the street looking for that familiar mustard coloured camel coat but he was gone. I started to doubt my own mind – maybe I had imagined he was there, maybe he wasn't at all. My heart was racing and I felt palpitations, I swear you could hear the blood rushing around my body as I ran up and down the little narrow lanes near the cottage. It wasn't long before I found myself at the promenade and I stood leaning over the old wrought iron bar. Looking over to the cave, I knew that I needed to go over to it and try to get home, as soon as the sea went out and the pathway was safe.

Chapter Eight

The Time Toucher

I became aware that there was someone standing quite close to me and I turned to find in utter disbelief the stranger standing there with me smiling.

"Don't be alarmed, petal," he said, reminiscent to the time he spoke to me on the train which in all honesty felt like a whole lifetime ago. "I am sure you are very frightened and have lots of questions. I remember the first time it happened to me, and I was terrified."

"It's you, you were on the train with me, you gave me my pen, and you helped the old lady, you ...." I said, blabbing out everything at once.

"Yes it's me, my name is Benjamin John Robert, or Ben for short, and you are?"

"I am Cassie," I said, keen to move on to my next question.

"How am I here in Cowes over a hundred years before I was even born, before my parents were born? How are you here? How can I get home? What happened, was it the wishing bench? My letter in the bottle?" I kept spurting out question after question and I was not even giving him the opportunity to answer any of them. My speech was becoming faster and my heart began racing again.

"There is lots to tell you, my dear Cassie, some of your questions I will have answers to and others you will have to find out for yourself, we all do."

"We?" I said, confused.

"Yes, all of us, you and I are not the only ones with our 'gift'."

Ben suggested we went for a short walk and sat on a park bench near an old bandstand in the local park, not far from the promenade.

"We are 'Time Touchers', Cassie," said Ben, looking at my inquisitive face.

"What? What's a 'Time Toucher'?"

"We find things, dropped, lost or stolen from people who have an impact on our world, our history and it is our destiny to return them to them and in doing so we preserve history, we are in fact responsible for it."

"I have no idea what you are talking about. What do you mean? I haven't found anything and returned it," I said, dismissive of his explanation.

"You dropped your pen at some point in time, I happened to be on my way to work, I had just picked up a newspaper and decided to sit and read it on the old seat in Brew, when I looked down and saw something protruding from the soil underneath. I should have known better. I had taken off my gloves to turn the pages of the newspaper, so I thought I was in no danger."

"Danger?" I said, needing to know more.

"Yes we wear our gloves to protect us from touching objects, things that can transport us back in time. I saw the tip of the pen and started to dig it out, I had not realised it had been there for years. The peat had preserved it and it looked as new as the day you dropped it, no doubt."

"But I must have dropped it that day you returned it to me, on the train, I must have done for you to find it and give me it back?" I was confused as I was saying it but then I thought about it. I met the gentleman on the train from home not in Brew. I had used the pen at the old wishing seat when I was in Brew yet the gentleman had given me it back the day before I used it!

He then went on to tell me that he had picked the pen up, put it in his pocket and continued his day at work; it was not until he got on the train to go home that he realised as he walked down the carriage he had gone back in time. He then spotted me and knew he had to return the pen. It was his destiny to return it to me.

"What year are you from?" I asked.

"2097."

So like me he was from the future? Only he was from my future?

So he had explained that Time Touchers like me would find things and by touching them you would be transported in time to meet the person who had lost it, for some important but unknown reason, to preserve history and help them fulfil their destiny.

Well that explained why he was on the train with me in 2017, but not how he had ended up in Cowes with me over a hundred years earlier.

"I have no idea," he said. "I am as confused as you are. It was 2097 when I boarded the train, 2017 whilst on it and as I alighted I expected it to still be 2017, until I could find a way to get back to my time. Once you return the item to the owner it's then a case of finding a way to get back to your own time. Instead I end up here with you in 1904."

But what item had I found that belonged to someone? What made me time travel?

"That's it, I found your handkerchief!" Getting it out

of my jeans pocket, "you must have dropped it getting off the train and I found it, here," I said, handing him back the blood stained handkerchief.

"But that doesn't explain how I am in 1904? Or how you are? If you are from my future does it?" I said, confused.

"No," said Ben, "but it does explain how I am still with you and I have travelled back with you to help you fulfil your destiny. By finding and touching my handkerchief the bond has not been broken, not until you return it to me."

So if it was not the handkerchief, what was it that had transported me back in time? I couldn't think, there was nothing!

"So is that why you wear gloves? Even on a hot, sunny day?" I asked.

"It is, Cassie, but I have found over the years, if it is your destiny to help another you cannot cover up fate."

"So why has it happened to me? Why you?" I asked, needing the answers to my questions.

"I believe it is hereditary. Not in every generation but it is passed down the genetic line."

As he said the words, it all made sense...Pops.

He had always worn gloves from as far back as I could remember, even on a hot day. I had thought he had a skin complaint or had a weird obsession but now it all started to make sense. He always made me wear them when we went out metal detecting and the way he got upset with me when I asked to touch his antiquities that were all behind lock and key. He was protecting me in case I had been given the 'Gift'.

"My grandfather Pops, he wears gloves all the time, he must be a Time Toucher too." Ben nodded in agreement.

So the symbol, I thought, what was that all about?

It was on Ben's handkerchief, Ben had drawn it on the sand and yes, it was the same symbol I had seen so many times before. It was all fitting into place. I had dreamt about a weird symbol the night before I had left for Brew. When Austin's friend had spilled his drink on the pavement, the weird syrupy shape was formed. In Pop's antiquity cabinet, the old parchment had the symbol on it and finally on the old wishing bench engraved deep in the wood together with the letters R.E.M.E.M.B.E.R on it. It was me, it was written for me! I was the one that had to remember it.

"The symbol, Ben, the one you drew in the sand, the one on your handkerchief, what does it mean?"

"It is our sign, Cassie, it is the secret sign of 'Time Touchers'; it is there to try and help us, to help each other to fulfil our destiny and to get home."

"How do you know when you have fulfilled your

destiny, Ben?"

"You don't, Cassie, well not at the time, it's not obvious. It is only when you get back to your own time and you do some research into the person you met, you understand why you were needed and how you made an impact on their lives.

"We are the unsung heroes, Cassie, that is our role in this life. We are protectors of humanity and no one will ever know, we will never get recognition, it is our secret."

"Who have you helped? Where have you been?" I asked Ben. My imagination was running wild thinking of all the great famous people throughout the centuries.

"We are not allowed to talk about it, Cassie, not even to each other. We do not want to change history, it could be dangerous."

I thought about everything I had been told; it was a lot to take in but now that I knew everything I was able to accept my fate – after all isn't that what I had wished for in my letter in a bottle only days earlier?

Ben and I sat chatting and I noticed he was keen not to talk about the time he was from, I was not allowed to have a sneak preview of the future.

"So how do you get home? Back to the time we came from?" I asked the one question I really needed the answer to, the most important answer.

"When you least expect it, Cassie, when your deed is done," he said, smiling.

Ben accompanied me back to the cottage and we agreed a time to meet later that day. Walking into the cottage I had some answers but not all. Why had I been transported back to 1904? And who was I supposed to help?

Chapter nine

A job well done

Annie, Barnes and John had not even realised I was awake and out of the bedroom so were shocked as I walked into the drawing room.

I was keen to speak to Barnes by himself. Obviously I was conscious knowing I had to be careful not to talk about history or to him it would be the future. It was 1904, there were to be two world wars, numerous natural disasters and assassinations of very important people in the world.

The maid brought in some tea and cakes and we all sat and enjoyed the much needed refreshments.

Annie went away then came back with some very old traditional games. There were marbles, a game which involved dice and a game where you used string, something like 'cat's cradle'.

"Let's play," said an excited Annie. She was such a lovely sweet girl; it was lovely spending time with her. In fact with all of them really. John was quiet but very sweet and very clever. Barnes was my saviour, strong, sensible and reliable, the kind of person who you wanted to spend time with, so interesting.

After we played the parlour games I looked over at the clock. It was almost 3.30 and the time I had agreed to meet Ben again.

"Barnes, would you like to come with me to meet my uncle?" I asked, giving a slight, secret wink.

"Your uncle? Oh yes of course, Cassie, I would be honoured," said Barnes, confused but all the time playing along with me.

Annie continued to play the games with John; he was such a lovely brother, always showing such time and patience for his sister. Both he and Barnes were brilliant brothers. I felt very envious but at the same time proud to have met them.

As Barnes and I left to go and meet "my Uncle" or Ben in reality, I was keen to tell him about our meeting.

I told him how I was a 'Time Toucher', how I had met Ben, how he had found my pen and was transported back into my time. Then how he was unable to get back home because he had dropped his handkerchief and I, another

'Time Toucher', had picked it up, bringing him back into the past with me. I told him about the symbol, which was a kind of sign, a secret symbol to help other 'Time Touchers' like myself.

Barnes was amazing, he took all the information in his stride; he did not seem shocked or surprised. I guess having such a scientific brain he was open to accepting the unknown, the impossible.

"Thank you, Barnes you are an incredible friend, you have never doubted me or thought I was mad."

"Cassie, everything is IMPOSSIBLE until it becomes POSSIBLE," he said and now I totally understood why he was such a keen inventor.

We walked up to where I had arranged to meet Ben at the little bench in the park. As we waited I described the symbol on the old wishing bench at home and how the word remember was carved into it. He seemed to just listen and take everything in, never once asking me any awkward questions that he knew I would be unable to answer.

We had sat for over an hour and Ben had not turned up. I felt I needed him to turn up to validate my story. I felt as though Barnes believed me but without actually meeting Ben and talking to him there was no proof I was telling the truth.

"Maybe he has gone back to his time, Cassie; he has fulfilled his destiny on this occasion," said Barnes.

Funny when those words came from him it didn't sound ludicrous at all. It sounded totally believable.

The thought hadn't entered my head, but he must be right which meant I was alone again and with no one to answer any more of my questions.

I had to figure out how I got here. I would not know the reason why until I got back home and to my own time.

"Ben said I must have found something from the past, from 1904 and been transported back to return it to its rightful owner but I haven't found anything? I remember finding Ben's handkerchief but he was from the future.

"I really don't think I'm ever going to get home to Brew at this rate," I said, as my eyes started to fill up with tears again.

"Don't worry, Cassie, we will figure this out together, we need to retrace your steps from when you left your home until you got here. I promise I will help you, I always will try and help you even if it means spending my life trying," said Barnes. Taking my hand he smiled at me and I was so thankful I had found a good friend who would help me fulfil my destiny.

We headed back to the cottage and as we approached

we saw Annie and John waving at the window, pleased to see us.

It was a lovely day so we decided to sit in the garden. There were beautiful flowers all over and the trees were in full bloom. Annie came to join us whilst we sat and had lemonade. It was not lemonade like I knew it, it was made with freshly squeezed lemons and it was so bitter.

The maid had been washing the clothes in the laundry room and she came into the garden with a basket of freshly washed clothes ready to hang up to dry in the warm sun.

My mind drifted back and I wondered about Ben – where had he gone? Had he returned back to his time? If so he must have fulfilled his purpose, with me?

Barnes could see I was looking melancholy and he smiled at me, a knowing smile, and a smile to let me know I was not alone.

Annie was sitting picking daisies and started to make a daisy chain. "I've made a bracelet for you, Cassie," she said with a wonderful, cheerful smile, handing me the delicate bracelet. I carefully put it on to show my appreciation. "It's beautiful, Annie; you're so kind, thank you."

I got up and sat with Annie on the grass and picked up a golden buttercup. Putting it under Annie's chin, I said, laughing, "You like butter!"

"Yes I do," said an excited Annie.

By this time John had come to join us with a model plane, which prompted Barnes to go and get his.

As the boys flew their planes this way and that, the maid continued to hang out the washing.

Suddenly something caught my eye from where she was standing and it made me look over. There on the ground lay the plane pin.

It had obviously been washed whilst still in the shorts pocket and had fallen out when the maid put them on the line.

I bent down to pick up the pin and that's when I saw it, the strange swirly symbol engraved on its wing. My symbol.

"That's it, Barnes, that's it!" I screamed in realisation.

"What's it?"

"The pin, your pin! I found that in the cave, in my time, before I ended up here! Don't you see that's the object that was lost and the object I found, I touched, why I ended up here!"

Barnes looked at me and took the pin from my hand looking at it closely. Still looking puzzled he swept his thumb over the etched symbol and then looked up.

"If you're right, Cassie, then that means you were

brought back in time to help me. You SAVED MY LIFE. It also means that you have fulfilled your destiny and you may be able to go home like Ben."

Could he be right? I thought back to Ben, how had he helped me? Was it the fact he told me I am a 'Time Toucher'?

Then I remembered Ben's words, "You will never know why you were needed, Cassie, not until you return home and do some research – only then you will understand your importance in history."

John and Annie were totally oblivious of our conversation, still doing their own things.

If that was it, that I had saved Barnes's life days earlier, why was I still here?

"I am going to the beach, anyone want to come?" said John. "You need the wind at the shoreline to get a real distance flying these," he added, holding up his model aircraft.

"Yes, John, I'm in," I said soon followed by the agreement of Barnes and Annie.

Picking up my bag, I set off towards the beach. As we walked Barnes and I held back to walk together, to talk.

"You know, Cassie, I promise I will not tell a soul about you, about 'Time Touchers' and I promise if I can help you any time in the future, I will. Look out for your symbol and remember me." Sadness came over him because we both knew what going home really meant. In my time Barnes would no longer be alive and I would never see him ever again.

As we got to the beach John started to fly his planes and Annie started to collect shells and stones. She began to try and throw the stones like I had done a couple of days before but with no success. With each throw they sunk into the deep water, not skimming once. Barnes got his sketch book out and watched his sister, sketching and drawing arrows and writing down strange equations.

I got up and picked up some stones and stood with Annie.

"Look, Annie, try again, you can do it," I said, showing her the angle to throw the stone.

Barnes, who had tried a few days earlier, got up and joined us. Picking up a stone he examined it and like when you see the athletes prepare to run just before the whistle goes, he got himself ready to throw. The first couple of attempts failed but then finally with a great roar bouncing from wave to wave to a remarkable distance flew his stone. Skipping from wave to wave, bouncing like a bouncing ball, the stone danced on the ocean waves, skimming into history. It is hard to think a simple game that day helped to save a world...but it did.

"That's it!" said Barnes and what followed had me totally lost as he explained the mathematical reason why the stone had glided together with the physics involved.

"Can we have an ice cream?" said Annie, bringing her clever brother down to earth. Barnes put his hand in his pocket and gave his brother John some coins asking him to go over to the little shop next to the promenade and bring back some for everyone. Annie went with him to carry the delicious delights.

Barnes kept on throwing his stones, keen to perfect his technique.

Picking up one of John's planes I began to fly it, keen to see how far I could get it. Barnes was in a world of his own and didn't notice me go over towards the cave to collect John's plane which had flown a great distance. As I went to collect the plane I stepped into the entrance of the cave looking for where the plane had landed. I could not see it anywhere.

After a few minutes of searching I resolved myself to the fact that I had lost his plane – it must have fallen onto the shore just before the entrance to the cave and been taken out to sea by the tide which was going out.

I came out of the cave and the first thing I noticed was the beach. It was not shingle anymore, it was golden, soft sand.

Then I saw it looking up to the horizon, there high on the mound was the 'Wishing bench'. I was home!

I ran along the shore and up the mound, keen to sit on the seat, keen to touch it, keen to make sure I wasn't imagining it. Sitting on the seat, I looked at the engraved etchings on the back. REMEMBER and the symbol, my symbol.

I thought back to Pops when I had asked him about the seat, how old it was, who put it there and his words echoed in my mind. "It's been here as long as I can remember, Cassie, it was put here by some famous inventor who loved Brew and loved sitting here looking at the beautiful scenery."

Barnes. It was Barnes. He had said he would try to help me in the future and he tried, putting the seat here and engraving the word REMEMBER on it with my symbol.

"I will always try and help you, Cassie, even in the future look for the symbol and remember." Barnes's words flew into my mind and I knew. He had kept his promise and put this seat here for me to try and help me.

I thought about him, John and Annie. How I had just disappeared and how I would be gone when they came back with the ice creams. How he would have had to make up a story probably something like I had gone back to my uncle's, how I had asked him to say goodbye for me.

I then thought about Nan and Pops, Mum and Dad and all my friends at school, Phoebe, Austin, Jenson and how I had been missing for days, how they would be worried about me.

I stood up and turned my hand putting it to my mouth as I kissed the palm of my hand then placed it on the etched word and symbol. "Thank you, Barnes," I whispered, hoping that he knew I knew he had fulfilled his promise.

Running as fast as I could to Nan's house I ran into the back door so out of breath I could hardly stand. There dressed in her frilly apron stood Nan at the kitchen stove and in the corner sitting at the table was Pops completing a crossword in the newspaper and sitting with his favourite mug, drinking black tea. No one was allowed to wash his mug because it 'spoiled the taste of the tea'.

They both looked shocked as I ran in. "I'm home, I'm back!" I said, grabbing my Nan and holding her so tight, never wanting to let her go.

"Cassie, my dear, what's wrong? We have only been away a few hours into town. When we got back you were not here but the kettle was still warm so we knew you had just popped out," said a reassuring Nan.

I looked over to Pops and he could see by my dazzled,

wide look in my eyes that something had happened.

I let go of Nan and went over to where Pops was sitting and as I did, taking his pen he drew on the side of the paper. As I sat down he held my hand and took it over to touch the thing he had just drawn. The symbol, our symbol.

He looked at me not saying a word and I just nodded.

Nan carried about her daily tasks muttering to herself and Pops and I went into the lounge.

We sat for a while and talked. He explained like Ben had done over a hundred years earlier that he too was a 'Time Toucher' and that although he never knew if it had been hereditary, passed down the line, he had suspected I had the gift. He explained why he made me wear gloves and how he too had had many adventures although not going into any specific details. I wanted to tell him about Barnes, Annie and John, about Ben but he stopped me at each attempt reminding me we were forbidden to talk about it even to each other.

After our talk, he gave me a huge, all encompassing, tight cuddle and walked into the kitchen answering Nan's calls for help in dishing out the vegetables for tea.

On the table next to me was my iPad. Picking it up I went on line, my fingers almost too scared to type into the search engine.

Barnes Wallis... Born on 26th September 1887 in Ripley Derbyshire, he had a brother John and sister Annie. The boys liked to make paper aeroplanes and toys for in his workshop. Had an apprenticeship in Cowes and went on to be a major inventor.

Barnes Wallis invented the drum shaped rotating bomb that could bound over water and was used in the famous 'Dam Busters' operation in May 1943, during the Second World War. Bound over water...bounce from wave to wave without sinking like a pebble skimming and dancing on the sea. So there it was: my reason, my destiny fulfilled. I smiled reading about what an extraordinary life he had had; I was so proud to have known him.

As I looked around the room I thought about all the adventures I had yet to come. Where would they take me? Who would I meet?

Looking at my coat or arms above the fireplace, the gloved hand, it all made sense.

TEMPUS FUGIT...
TIME FLIES.